# The Strange Case of Dr. Jekyll and Mr. Hyde

Abridged English Classics

# The Strange Case of Dr. Jekyll and Mr. Hyde

### Robert Louis Stevenson

ibs BOOKS (UK)

**The Strange Case of Dr. Jekyll and Mr. Hyde**
Stevenson,Robert Louis

English Classics Series

© Publisher

ISBN : 978-1-905863-16-7

Price in India : Rs. 125/-

This Edition : 2015

Published by
**ibs BOOKS (UK)**
Suite 4b, Floor 15, Wembley Point,
1 Harrow Road, Wembley HA9 6DE (U.K.)
www.foreignlanguagebooks.co.uk

Printed in India

# Index

# About the Author

Robert Lewis Stevenson was born in Edinburgh, Scotland, on November 13, 1850. His father, Thomas Stevenson, and his grandfather, Robert Stevenson were both distinguished lighthouse designers and engineers. It was from them that Stevenson inherited his love of adventure and the joy of the sea.

He was a sickly child and had respiratory problems throughout his life. Stevenson's father wanted his son to become a lighthouse designer and engineer too. But Stevenson himself was far more interested in building up wonderful romances and tales of adventure in his mind. As a young man, Stevenson travelled through Europe and wrote two travel narratives. In 1876, Stevenson fell in love with a married woman, Fanny Van de Grift

Osbourne, who eventually divorced her husband and married Stevenson.

Over the next decade Stevenson wrote three books that became hugely popular and earned much success and admiration. First of these was *Treasure Island* which was written in 1883. This was followed by *Kidnapped* in 1886. Both these books were adventure stories. *Treasure Island* was a pirate tale full of daring and thrilling adventures. *Kidnapped* was a historical novel set in Stevenson's native Scotland. These two books were followed by the work that earned Stevenson even greater fame and success. This was *The Strange Case of Dr. Jekyll and Mr. Hyde*, which came out in 1886. It met with tremendous success, sold over 40,000 copies in six months and ensured Stevenson recognition as a writer of great merit and capabilities.

By the late 1880s, Stevenson had become one of the most celebrated names of English literature. But his health continued to trouble him. His later days were racked by the misery of tuberculosis. At about this time, Stevenson decided to settle in Samoa. It was here that the famous writer breathed his last. He died of a brain haemorrhage on December 3, 1894 at the age of forty-four.

# One

## **Story Of The Door**

$M$ r. John Gabriel Utterson was an honest and kind hearted lawyer. He was a very serious man who smiled rarely and had a dusty and dull appearance. However, despite being a stern and austere man himself, Utterson never resented merriment and cheerfulness in others. His goodness reflected from the way he was always ready to help the people in need and to solve their problems instead of criticizing them.

It was, however, not easy to win Mr. Utterson's friendship. This wise and prudent lawyer befriended only those people whom he knew well and considered worthy of his regard. Richard Enfield was one such friend. Enfield was also a cousin of Mr. Utterson and was a carefree and lively young man. The two men used to meet every Sunday and liked going out for long walks.

Once, while they were enjoying just such a walk, they happened to wander into a street in a busy area of London. It was Sunday and so the street was quieter than usual in the absence of the weekdays' rush and traffic. It was a very nice and clean lane with well painted shutters, polished brass fittings and lovely, well kept houses and shops lining its borders. And as the two men walked into it, they considered it quite a pleasant place in comparison to the dirty surrounding streets.

But even in this nice and clean place there was a house that stood out sharply in contrast, thanks to its stained exterior that showed negligence and disuse. It was two storeys high and had not even a single window on the ground floor. There was only a dirty door that had neither a bell on it nor any kind of a knocker.

The two men looked at this door and Mr. Enfield asked, "Have you ever noticed this door before?" Mr. Utterson nodded to indicate that he had. "It always reminds me of a very strange incident," Mr. Enfield added.

"Really? What kind of incident?" Mr. Utterson asked.

"Well, what happened was so strange that it still confuses me," Mr. Enfield said. "It was around three o'clock one cold winter morning. I was returning from a party and just happened to pass through this street. I noticed two figures. One of them was a short man walking quite rapidly. The other was a young girl, about eight years old I think. She was running in from the opposite direction. Both collided into each other and the girl fell down. But what shocked me was that instead of helping the child up, the man trampled on her and left her sprawled on the road. The poor child was screaming with pain and yet the man didn't bother. I couldn't bear it, so I ran towards the man, caught hold of him and dragged him back to where the child was lying. The little girl's family had arrived by that time. Several other people also gathered at the spot and somebody called a doctor. The nasty man whom I had caught and brought back to the injured girl stood quietly and watched everything without seeming least bothered.

Fortunately, the child wasn't much hurt. And the matter would have ended there. But that man had such a wicked look on his face that I began to sweat despite the coldness. Even the doctor that had been called looked horrified after having one look at the man. Everybody felt angry at what the villain had done. And what added to our anger was that the culprit himself hardly seemed bothered. No word passed between the crowd gathered there, but instantly we all decided that that man needed to be punished. He had such an awful look on his face that we really felt like hitting him or even killing him on the spot. But of course that was not an option. So we decided to make him pay. As the crowd started getting angry and threatened him, he relented and agreed to give some money as compensation to the girl's family.

"I'm a gentleman and I don't want to create any scene or scandal. If you think I did some wrong then I'm ready to pay whatever price you think fit as compensation," he said.

"We all decided that the man must pay up at least a hundred pounds to the girl's family. Can you imagine what followed next? How he gave us the money?"

"No, I can't imagine," Mr. Utterson replied.

"Well, the rogue made us all walk up to this very door," said Mr. Enfield. "He took out a key, opened the door and went in. He came back after some time and handed us ten pounds in cash. For the rest, he gave us a cheque drawn on Coutts' bank. I looked at the cheque and realized that the signature on it was of a well known person. I cannot tell you whose signature it was, but trust me that it was of someone very important. I immediately became suspicious. It looked quite strange to see a mean looking man walk into a cellar and come out with a cheque for ninety pounds bearing another man's signature. And it was very late too, nearly four in the morning."

"What happened after that?" asked Mr. Utterson.

"Well, the villain offered to stay with us till the bank opened and the cheque could be encashed. So I, that man and some other people, all decided to wait in my room till that time. In the morning, we went to the bank and I presented the cheque myself, indicating in clear terms that I suspected the signature on the cheque to be forged. But imagine my surprise when I was told that the signature was genuine!"

"Oh, really?" Mr. Utterson exclaimed.

"Yes, the signature was genuine and so was the cheque. But I still can't understand how."

"May I ask you a question, Enfield?"

"Sure, what?" Mr. Enfield said.

"What was the name of that man who walked over the child," Mr. Utterson said.

"Sure, I can tell you his name. It was a man of the name of Hyde," Mr. Enfield said.

"Hyde?" Mr. Utterson repeated.

"Yes, he called himself Hyde. And yet the cheque was signed by a very well known man whom everybody considers very respectable. I simply cannot imagine what these two people have to do with each other.

One seems to be such a bad character while the other is virtuous and good."

"Did you try to find out if the drawer of the cheque lives in that house?"

"No, he doesn't," Mr. Enfield replied. "I read the address on the cheque, it was not of that house. Evidently, the drawer of the cheque lives somewhere else. I didn't make many enquiries but I have studied that strange house where Hyde had taken us. It doesn't have any other entry except that dirty door and I've heard that nobody except Mr. Hyde goes in and out of that door. In fact, even he himself is a rare visitor to that house. The ground floor has no windows as you might have noticed. There are three windows on the upper floor, but they always remain closed. However, the chimney of the house is generally smoking, so it's obvious that somebody does live there."

"What kind of man is this Mr. Hyde?" Mr. Utterson asked.

"Oh, all I can say is that there is something very wrong with his appearance; something very displeasing and detestable. I've never seen a man before whom I disliked with such intensity. And I don't even know why I disliked him. He's very strange. I mean, Hyde is not ugly, and I can't really point out anything wrong as far as his appearance is concerned. But there's something about him that is hateful and disturbing. Perhaps, the man is deformed in some way, but I'm not sure. The only thing I'm sure about is that he's repulsive and revolting."

"Alright. Now tell me this, are you sure that Hyde used a key when he opened that door?" Mr. Utterson asked.

"Of course I'm sure, but why did you ask?" Mr. Enfield said.

Mr. Utterson twitched his lips and looked a bit thoughtful. "Well, my dear Enfield," he said after a moment, "it might seem strange to you but I already know the name of the person whose signature was there on that cheque. That's why I didn't ask you who that person was, because I know it already. Therefore I'd request you to think again and tell me for sure whether everything that you have just told me is absolutely correct."

"You should have told me earlier that you already knew the name of that respectable person whose signature was there on the cheque. But I have not told you anything wrong. It all happened exactly as I told you. Mr. Hyde had a key with which he opened that door. He still has it. I saw him using it just a week ago."

Two

# Search For Mr. Hyde

That evening when Mr. Utterson returned to his home, he seemed disturbed and worried. He had his dinner and then, instead of sitting down to some quiet reading as was his usual routine, he went into his study. He quickly opened up his business safe and picked up a long envelope endorsed as Dr. Jekyll's Will. Mr. Utterson pursed his lips as he looked at it. He had agreed to take charge of the will and keep it safe even though he had strictly refused to assist in making it. The will dictated that in case of the death of Dr. Henry Jekyll, M.D., D.C.L., L.L.D., F.R.S., etc., all his possessions were to pass into the hands of his "friend and benefactor Edward Hyde". The will also directed that "in the case of unexplained disappearance or absence of Dr. Jekyll for any period exceeding three calendar months," Edward Hyde was to take charge of all properties belonging to Dr. Jekyll without any condition except to pay small amounts to Dr. Jekyll's servants.

Mr. Utterson had always disliked this will. He considered it insane and strange enough to make him suspicious. Dr. Jekyll was his friend. But the lawyer had never heard about this stranger called Mr. Edward Hyde. Not until that evening. What Mr. Enfield had told him that evening had only made Mr. Utterson feel more worried. According to Mr. Enfield, the man called Hyde was a wicked and hateful person. What the lawyer could not understand was how Dr. Jekyll, a very good and kindly person, had found himself indebted, in any way, to a nasty person like Hyde.

The concerned lawyer carefully read the will again and then put it back in the safe. "I must find out the truth," he muttered to himself as he began to dress. "And the only person who can know anything about the matter is Lanyon. I must go and talk to him." With this thought in his mind, Mr. Utterson quickly walked out of his home to visit his friend Dr. Lanyon.

Dr. Lanyon was an old friend of Mr. Utterson as well as Dr. Jekyll. They had been school and college mates and respected and trusted each other with utmost sincerity. Dr. Lanyon was a robust gentleman with a hearty manner and loud resounding laugh. His locks of white hair, red face and open and generous nature made him quite a pleasing person to be with. He welcomed Mr. Utterson cordially.

After talking a little about general matters, Mr. Utterson raised the issue that was disturbing him. He started talking about Dr. Jekyll and said, "We two are the oldest friends Dr. Henry Jekyll has, isn't it?"

"Yes, but I wish we were the youngest friends he had!" Dr. Lanyon laughed. "But yes, we have known him and been his friends longer than anybody else I suppose. But I scarcely see Jekyll these days."

"Same with me. But I had hoped you'd have been more in touch with Jekyll. You two had similar interests," Mr. Utterson said.

"Yes, we had," the doctor replied. "But in

the recent years, Henry Jekyll became just too fanciful for me. I still care about him because he is an old friend. But I hardly see him nowadays. I fear Henry has developed some kind of mental problem. He has started thinking up all kinds of bizarre ideas, and most unscientific ones too."

"But did you ever hear him mention any friend of his called Edward Hyde?" Mr. Utterson put forward the question he had come to ask.

"Edward Hyde? No, I never heard that name before. If this Edward Hyde is a friend of Jekyll's then he must be a recent acquaintance."

Mr. Utterson realized with disappointment that Dr. Lanyon knew even less about Hyde than himself. He returned to his home feeling even more worried than before. The strange matter had disturbed him so much that he couldn't sleep at night and kept on tossing and turning in his bed. Whatever Mr. Enfield had told kept on passing through his mind. He closed his eyes but instead of sleeping he started seeing the things Mr. Enfield had told him about. The troubled lawyer saw the cold winter night, the sinister figure of Mr. Hyde walking quickly and also the little child running. Mr. Utterson could almost hear the pattering sound of her feet as she gaily ran down the street. Then he saw the horrible sight of the villain trampling on the fallen child and leaving her screaming and in pain.

Often during that night, Mr. Utterson also imagined his friend Dr. Jekyll sleeping peacefully in his nice and comfortable home. The door would open and a menacing form would enter his room, overcoming Dr. Jekyll and controlling the kind and respectable man with its sinister power. It was a horrible thing to imagine, and quite worrying too. The dark, menacing form kept on troubling the lawyer all night. Every time he dozed off, he dreamt of the ominous form trampling over little children and leaving them crying and screaming on the cold streets. But the dark figure Mr. Utterson kept on seeing in his dream had no face since the lawyer didn't know what Mr. Hyde looked like.

But Utterson was curious to know. He

wanted to see the real Mr. Hyde and to judge for himself whether the man was really as evil as he sounded from the description of Mr. Enfield. Mr. Utterson felt sure that if he could just see the real Hyde, see his face, then he would not feel so troubled about the matter. Perhaps, just by meeting Mr. Hyde it might be possible to determine why Dr. Jekyll felt so attached to him to have dictated such a surprising will. If nothing else, it would still be worth seeing a face that had shaken a calm and reasonable man like Mr. Enfield.

"I must find this Mr. Edward Hyde, whoever he is. He may be Mr. Hyde, but I can also be Mr. Seek!" the lawyer determined. So, from the next day Mr. Utterson started visiting the strange house from where Mr. Hyde had brought out the cheque. He watched it from the street corner. He went there in the morning before going to work and then again in the afternoon. Even at night, the lawyer kept his watch in the hope of catching a sight of the mystery that Mr. Hyde was.

It was only after several days that Mr.

Utterson caught sight of a person resembling the man Mr. Enfield had described. It was a clear night and there was a bit of chill in the air. It was quite late so all the shops were closed and the street bore a deserted look. An eerie silence hung in the air, unbroken except for the distant hum of the London City. The street lamps did what they could to spread some light on the road. Mr. Utterson waited and watched from a secluded corner, hoping that at least that night he would be able to see the person he had been waiting for. Suddenly, some footsteps broke through the silence of the night air. The person who was approaching the street was still far off but from the sound of his footsteps Mr. Utterson could easily make out that he was walking heavily and unsteadily.

The lawyer felt sure that the approaching person was Mr. Hyde. He quickly hid himself in the dark courtyard of the very house into which he knew Hyde would enter.

The footsteps kept on coming closer and closer. Mr. Utterson remained hidden and waiting. Soon he could see a figure approaching the house. The lawyer could see that the person was a short, plainly dressed man. But he could not see the stranger's face. The man went straight to the door and drawing a key from his pocket began to open it.

Mr. Utterson immediately stepped out of the shadow and tapped the stranger on the shoulder. "Excuse me, but are you Mr. Hyde?" he asked.

The stranger took a quick step away with a hissing intake of breath. But he quickly recovered. He kept his face turned away but answered in an easy manner, "Yes, my name is Mr. Hyde. What do you want from me?"

"You are going in perhaps, to meet Dr. Jekyll. May I come with you too? My name is Mr. Utterson and I'm an old friend of Dr. Jekyll. You must have heard of me," Mr. Utterson calmly answered.

"Dr. Jekyll is not at home," Mr. Hyde said. "But how did you know my name?"

"Will you do me a favour?" Mr. Utterson asked without bothering to answer Hyde's question.

"Sure, with pleasure. What do you want me to do?"

"Nothing much, I just want to see your face. Would you show me your face?" Mr. Utterson asked.

The man standing before the lawyer hesitated for a moment. Then he suddenly turned and looked directly at Mr. Utterson.

"Thank you, it was only so I could know you the next time we meet. That's all."

"Okay, I too think it's good that we have met," Mr. Hyde replied. "You can have my address too," saying this he gave a number of a street in Soho. "And now that I've done what you wanted, would you tell me how you knew my name?"

"Somebody had described you to me," the lawyer answered.

"Who?"

"We have common friends," said Mr. Utterson.

"Common friends?" echoed Mr. Hyde, a little hoarsely. "Who are they?"

"Jekyll, for instance," said the lawyer.

"Liar!" snarled Mr. Hyde. "Dr. Jekyll never told you anything about me. I did not expect that you would lie!"

"Oh come on, I'm not lying. It was only through Dr. Jekyll that I came to know about you," Mr. Utterson quickly said.

Mr. Hyde gave a short laugh and quickly opened the door. In just a moment he had entered the house and closed the door shut after him.

The shocked lawyer had no other choice but to walk down the street and go back. All the way he kept on thinking about Mr. Hyde. Utterson agreed with Mr. Enfield that Mr. Hyde was unpleasant and nasty. But it was not just because of his appearance. It was true that Mr. Hyde looked very pale and was quite short too. But that doesn't make a person bad. He gave an impression of being deformed in some way. But Mr. Utterson hadn't noticed any obvious bodily defect. His voice was husky, whispering and broken too and he surely had a very unpleasant smile. Those were all negative points, but the lawyer felt sure that there was something else that had made him feel disgusted and scared when in the presence of Mr. Hyde.

"There's something very wrong with that man. If only I knew what that something is! It's almost as if the evil of his soul and the wickedness of his heart radiates out from his body and scares those standing near him. Oh, Dr. Jekyll! What kind of a friend have you got yourself? If ever I saw a person who seemed like a Devil, it's Mr. Hyde!"

Mr. Utterson remained engrossed in such thoughts as he rounded the street corner and turned into a square of ancient houses. Some of these houses were in very bad condition. However, the second house from the corner looked grand and well kept. He turned to this house and knocked. The door was soon opened by a well-dressed elderly servant.

"Is Dr. Jekyll at home, Poole?" the lawyer asked.

"I'll go and see, Mr. Utterson. Please come in," Poole replied in most polite manner. He opened the door and led the lawyer into a large and luxuriously furnished hall. The open fire form the fireplace was spreading cheerful warmth in the room and the hall looked quite comfortable and welcoming. As Mr. Utterson looked around, he was reminded about the time when the hall had been a favourite place of gathering for Dr. Jekyll's friends. The elderly lawyer had himself considered it the most pleasant room in London.

However, Mr. Utterson was far too troubled to feel any pleasure that night. He still felt shaky and uneasy and very worried. Poole soon returned and told him that Dr. Jekyll was not at home at that time. Mr. Utterson felt ashamed of himself as he quickly realized that instead of being disappointed, he had in fact felt relieved to find Dr. Jekyll unavailable.

"Alright Poole," the lawyer replied. "But tell me something else. I just noticed Mr. Hyde going in by the old dissecting room door. Is he allowed to go into those rooms even in the absence of Dr. Jekyll?"

"Yes Sir," Poole replied. "Mr. Hyde has a key and Dr. Jekyll has also ordered us to obey all commands of Mr. Hyde."

"That shows how much your master trusts that young Mr. Hyde. But I'm surprised because I've never met him before," Mr. Utterson said.

"We too see very little of Mr. Hyde, Sir. He never dines here and doesn't come in this part of the house. He mostly comes in and goes out by the laboratory door," Poole replied.

Mr. Utterson nodded, wished Poole good night and stepped out of the house. He started walking back towards his home, feeling even more concerned and alarmed than before. He was sure now that his friend Dr. Jekyll was in some deep trouble.

"Perhaps something from his past has caught up with him. Dr. Jekyll must have done something wrong in his past and now this terrible Hyde has come to blackmail him!" Mr. Utterson muttered to himself.

"But this Mr. Hyde looks a villain too. He cannot have a very decent past either. I'm sure Hyde must have done many more terrible things than whatever mistake Dr. Jekyll had committed. But that is even more terrible. Hyde surely is a dangerous person. What if he learns about Dr. Jekyll's will? The rogue might kill the doctor just to get his dirty hands on all that money sooner! No, I cannot let that happen! I must help Jekyll. I would help him. But, what if he refuses to take my help?"

## Three

# Dr. Jekyll Was Quite At Ease

About fifteen days later, Dr. Jekyll invited some of his friends for a pleasant dinner party. It proved to be a cheerful evening, much like the old days. Mr. Utterson was invited to this party too. He took the opportunity to stay behind with Dr. Jekyll even after the party was over and all other guests had returned to their own homes.

Dr. Jekyll and Mr. Utterson sat down together after the party. They felt tired after the fun and gaiety. The elderly lawyer observed the doctor carefully as they sat face to face. Dr. Jekyll was a tall and well built man, about fifty years old. He was an intelligent and capable man with a kind and gentle look about him. Mr. Utterson had always liked him and considered him a dear friend. Dr. Jekyll thought the same about the lawyer too.

"I want to talk to you about something Jekyll," Mr. Utterson said after sometime. "It's about that will of yours."

Dr. Jekyll's expression made it clear that he did not quite like discussing the matter. But he managed to reply in a good natured way.

"Oh, Utterson, I know you don't like my will," Dr. Jekyll said. "Perhaps you think me insane for writing such a will. Well, Dr. Lanyon shares you view too. He harbours the same opinion about all my scientific views you know. But Lanyon is a good friend and really cares about me. The only thing is that he is really very stubborn about accepting new scientific ideas. He really disappoints me in that one point."

Mr. Utterson didn't care about the Jekyll's opinion about Dr. Lanyon's scientific views. "But you know Jekyll, I really don't approve of your will," he said instead.

"You don't approve of my will? Well, you have made that clear enough already," Dr. Jekyll said.

"And I'll say so again, I don't like it and I

don't approve of it," declared the lawyer. "I've been hearing about this Mr. Hyde of yours. And let me tell you, what I heard was not anything pleasant."

Dr. Jekyll turned pale and looked ill at ease. "I don't want to talk about it any more. Didn't I tell you before too that I don't want to discuss my will with any one?"

"But I've been hearing some very horrible things about Mr. Hyde," said Utterson.

"That won't make any difference to my will. You don't understand anything. The matters are very complicated. I'm caught in a tough situation and I can do nothing about it. So it's no use discussing the matter any further," Dr. Jekyll replied in a grim voice.

"But I'm your friend Jekyll. You can trust me, can't you?" Mr. Utterson protested. "Tell me what your problem is and I'd do everything to help you."

"I know I can trust you Utterson, and I'm much obliged too for your offer of help. I don't know how to thank you for your concern. I assure you that if ever I need help, I would seek you. I know you are my friend. But really the situation is not as bad as you perhaps imagine. I'm really not in need of any help. I can free myself of this Mr. Hyde anytime I want. But this is a private matter and I request you not to interfere in it."

"Well, in that case, I'll leave you alone with your friend Mr. Hyde. I'm sure you know well what is good for you," said Mr. Utterson as he got up from his chair and prepared to go.

"However, since we are talking about Hyde, I want you to know that I really care about that wretched man. I have really a very great interest in poor Hyde. I know you have already met him. He has told me everything. I fear he was rude to you. But I do sincerely take a great interest in that young man. And Utterson, I wish you to promise me that you will bear with him and get his rights for him after my death. I'm sure you would willingly do it, if you knew all the truth. But I cannot tell you everything. I can only request you to promise me that in case something happens to me, you'll help him,"

Dr. Jekyll said.

"I can scarcely bear that man. I don't like him at all," Mr. Utterson replied.

"That isn't necessary. I'm not asking you to like him. All I ask is that you be just with Hyde and help him get his due rights when I'm no longer here to take care of him."

Mr. Utterson sighed. "Alright, I promise," he said.

## Four

# A Murder Most Foul

I t was almost a year later when a savage crime shocked London. It was a crime of remarkable ferocity and terrified the hearts of those who heard about it.

The horrible thing happened one cold October night, at about 11 o'clock. At a house near the river, a maid servant had just entered into her bedroom. It was a bright and clear night so the young woman had lingered beside her window to look out a little at the pleasant night spread outside. She was looking down the street when she noticed a nice looking silver-haired gentleman walking down the road. She also saw a short and stubby man walking down from the other end of the road. The two men came close together near the maid's window. She saw the old man bow politely to the short man and seemed to be enquiring for an address. The maid didn't know who the gentleman was. But she was sure that the short man was Mr. Hyde. He had once visited her master. The girl recognized him instantly because she still remembered how hateful she had considered him to be even at the very first moment she had seen him.

The maid watched on with some curiosity and great anxiety. She saw Hyde listening to the old man with as much politeness as he was capable of. But it was clear to the girl that he was getting more and more impatient. Hyde carried a heavy stick in his hand which he was swinging in his impatience. Suddenly, he broke out into a fit of rage and began stamping his foot as if in fury and raising his cane in air like a madman. The old man stepped back in alarm. The very next moment Mr. Hyde started hitting the poor elderly gentleman with his stick. He pushed the old man to the ground and started trampling him, clubbing the helpless gentleman with his stick again and again. The maid was horrified to see the sight and fainted with terror.

It was about two o' clock when she regained her senses and called the police. The old gentleman lay dead in the middle of the road. There was no sign of his murderer though. Just a portion of his thick stick was found near the battered body. It was thick and strong and yet it had been broken by the intensity of the blows that had been showered upon the dead man. One part of it was discovered lying in the gutter by the road. The other half probably had been carried away by the cruel murderer.

A purse and a gold watch was also found near the body but no papers or card. There however was a long envelop in the pocket of the dead man bearing the name and address of Mr. Utterson.

A policeman carried the envelope to the lawyer early next morning and told him about the vicious crime that had taken place. The policeman asked Mr. Utterson whether he knew anything about the murder.

"I shall not be able to say anything till I have seen the body," the lawyer answered.

After getting dressed quickly and having a hurried breakfast, he accompanied the Police Officer to the Police Station. He was shown the dead body.

"Oh yes," Mr. Utterson exclaimed, "I recognize the body. It is Sir Danvers Carew."

"Oh my God!" the Police officer exclaimed too. "Are you sure Sir that the body is of Sir Danvers Carew? The case would be all over the news if it is so. I really hope you can help us catch the murderer too. Evidently it was some Mr. Hyde who committed the crime according to an eyewitness," the officer said and told the lawyer what the maid had seen at night.

The name of Hyde was enough in itself to disturb the lawyer. What made him even more anxious was the stick that Hyde had used to kill the old man. Mr. Utterson recognized it as the one he himself had gifted to Dr. Jekyll many years ago.

"Is this the same Hyde who is short in height?" he asked the Officer.

"Yes, the maid said that he's very small and very wicked looking as well," the Police

Officer replied.

"Well then, I can show you where he lives," Mr. Utterson said. He led the Officer to the Soho address that Mr. Hyde had given him. It was a dismal and grimy locality with muddy roads and ragged, ill mannered children roaming around in the streets. The locality had a menacing looking liquor bar, a French eating house and a bookstore selling cheap novels. It was not at all a place that might have been considered respectable in any way. And yet, it was in this very locality that the evidently favourite friend of Dr. Jekyll lived. A man whom everybody considered as evil and yet whom Dr. Jekyll had considered dear enough to make him the heir to the property worth a quarter million pounds.

The officer knocked at the door of the house mentioned in the address. A wicked looking old woman opened the door. She looked at the two respectable men standing at the door and immediately smoothed down her manners into what she considered to be polite. She told the officer that Hyde lived in that house but was out at that moment. She also said that he had returned very late the previous night and had gone out again within an hour of his return. The woman declared that such absences from the home was a regular habit of Mr. Hyde. She had seen him the previous day after a duration of two whole months.

"We would like to see Hyde's rooms," Mr. Utterson said letting the woman know that the man accompanying him was an inspector and so had full authority to search through anybody's rooms.

"Oh, so Hyde is in trouble, is he? What has he done now?" the woman asked with an obvious delight.

"That just shows that Hyde is just as unpopular here as in our parts," the inspector commented as they walked inside the house.

Mr. Hyde occupied only two rooms in the house. Both these rooms were richly and tastefully furnished. There was a closet in the corner of one of these rooms. It was full of choicest and most expensive wines. Everything else in the room boasted of luxury and wealth as well. However, both the rooms were in disarray and looked as if they had been recently ransacked. Clothes were strewn carelessly on the floor and several drawers stood open. In the fireplace there was a pile of ashes that showed that a lot of papers had recently been burned. From these ashes, the inspector recovered the remains of a partly burned chequebook. The inspector also found the other half of the stick from behind a door.

The lawyer and the inspector searched the room thoroughly but didn't find anything of much interest. However a trip to the bank told them that Mr. Hyde had several thousand pounds in his account.

"It shouldn't be difficult to catch this man," the inspector said. "He surely would come to the bank to withdraw his cash. All we have to do is to circulate his description in the bank so people could recognize him when he comes."

That however wasn't as easy as it seemed. Mr. Hyde didn't have any friends and even the people who had seen him could remember only that he was very short and made them feel scared and uneasy. Even the master of the maid who had witnessed the murder couldn't tell much as he had met Hyde only twice. Hyde had never been photographed and nobody had any idea about his family or his past life. Several people were asked but they all gave widely different descriptions. There was only one point on which everybody agreed. All those who described Hyde said that he gave them a sense of being deformed in some mysterious way.

Five

# **Incident Of The Letter**

M r. Utterson could not help but turn his steps once more to the house of Dr. Jekyll. Poole admitted him as before and led him down by the kitchen across a yard and towards a building which was known as the laboratory or the dissecting rooms. The house had once belonged to a famous surgeon who had used these rooms for his researches.

This was the first time that the lawyer was being received in these parts of his friend's house. He did not find it pleasurable or even interesting. The place was cold, eerily silent and strangely uncomfortable.

Mr. Utterson climbed up to the doctor's room. It was a large room fitted with glass panes and a business table. There were three windows in the room, all shuttered and dirty. A fire in the grate tried all it could to make the room a little warm and less uncomfortable. Dr. Jekyll was sitting near this fire looking sick and pale. He did not rise to welcome the lawyer but extended a hand to greet him. His hand felt strangely cold to Mr. Utterson and his voice sounded peculiar too.

"Have you heard the news Jekyll?" the lawyer immediately asked.

"People are shouting it all over the place. How can I have not heard it?" the doctor replied, becoming even more troubled at his friend's question.

"Carew was my client. He was a very respectable man and his untimely death bothers me a great deal. But you are my client too and a dear friend as well. I'm much more bothered by the thought of your danger. And I really need to know what you think about all this. I need to know this professionally as well as personally. You are not hiding this murderer or helping him in anyway, are you?" Mr. Utterson asked in a stern voice.

"No, I swear to God I'm not helping him,"

the doctor replied immediately. "I swear on my honour that I'll never see nor have anything to do with that man ever again! And there's no question of helping Hyde either. He doesn't need any help. Hyde is safe wherever he is. And believe me, he will never come back again."

Mr. Utterson didn't like the feverish manner in which Dr. Jekyll was saying all this. He looked gloomily at the doctor and said, "For your sake I too hope that Hyde never returns again. You know that if the case is brought to trial, your name might appear in it as well. You are the only person here who has befriended Hyde and even made him an heir of all your property. But what makes you so sure that he will not return?"

"I'm sure he would never return. But I cannot tell you what makes me so sure," Dr. Jekyll said, looking even more uncomfortable than before. "But there's something on which I want your advice. There's a letter I want to show you. I want you to tell me if I should show it to the police. I'll do as you advice me. I trust you completely and know that whatever you'd tell me would be for my best."

"Do you think that this letter might lead to Hyde's arrest?" Mr. Utterson asked.

"No, I don't care for Hyde, or what happens to him. I'm worried about myself and don't want to get into any unnecessary trouble," Dr. Jekyll answered.

This sounded as surprising selfishness to Mr. Utterson. But the lawyer was also relieved that his friend had finally started thinking about himself and how a friendship with a man like Hyde might affect his own reputation. Utterson asked the doctor to show him the letter.

The letter was written in a peculiar upright hand and was signed "Edward Hyde". It bore a message telling Dr. Jekyll not to fear for his friend Hyde's safety as he had a sure means of escape."

"Can I see the envelope too?" Mr. Utterson asked.

"I've already burnt it," Dr. Jekyll replied. "Besides, there was no postmark on it. It was hand delivered to me."

"I want to study this letter carefully so I shall keep it with me," the lawyer said.

"No problem, I trust you and know that you'll only give me good advice."

"Now tell me one more thing," Mr. Utterson said. "Was it Hyde who dictated the terms of your will, especially that part that makes him the owner of all your property in case of your disappearance?"

The doctor looked up at his friend and became even paler. He shuddered, pursed his lips and nodded.

"I knew it!" Mr. Utterson exclaimed. "Do you realize Jekyll that this Hyde of yours intended to murder you? You have had a fortunate escape."

"I know," Dr. Jekyll replied in a low voice. "And I've learnt a lesson too. An awfully bitter lesson!"

While walking out of the house, Mr. Utterson went over to Poole and asked him whether he had seen the messenger who had delivered the letter to Dr. Jekyll. Poole didn't know of the letter however. In fact, he felt sure no sort of letter had come that day except a few circulars that had come by post. This news alarmed Mr. Utterson even more. It was obvious that if the letter had not passed the servant's eyes, it must have come from the laboratory door. Perhaps, it was written from within the premises itself. And in that case, the letter indicated at much more than a successful escape of Hyde.

On his way back to his own home, Mr. Utterson heard the newsboys shouting, "Special edition. The Murder of an M.P." These sounds filled the lawyer's heart with gloom. Hyde had already killed one of his most respectable clients and a very good friend. The reputation and wellbeing of another was in danger because of the same man. And it disturbed the lawyer a great deal. He wished to help Dr. Jekyll but had no idea how to do that. The things were just too complicated and mysterious.

Soon after reaching his home, the lawyer summoned his head clerk, Mr. Guest. Guest had visited Dr. Jekyll's home on several occasions and was on familiar terms with Poole. More importantly, Guest was a student of handwriting and Mr. Utterson hoped that a detailed writing analysis of the letter Dr. Jekyll had given him might reveal some hidden secrets.

As soon as Mr. Guest arrived, the lawyer put the letter before him and told him to find out what he could from the writing of Hyde. "But don't tell about this to anyone. It should remain strictly between ourselves," he said.

Mr. Guest looked at the letter carefully. "Well, one thing is clear. This letter was not written by any mad or deranged man. But I admit that the writing is certainly very odd."

"That does not surprise me. The writer himself is a very odd man," Mr. Utterson said.

Just at that moment a servant entered the room with a note.

"May I see this note too Sir?" Mr. Guest asked when he heard that the note was from Dr. Jekyll.

"Sure, it's just a dinner invitation. You

can see it," Mr. Utterson replied handing the note to his clerk.

Mr. Guest spread out the note on a table alongside the letter he was already studying. He looked at the two papers for sometime and compared them carefully. "Hmm, this is very interesting," he said after few minutes.

"Why? What have you noticed?" Mr. Utterson asked.

"Well Sir, the writings on these papers have very particular similarities," the clerk replied. "There are many things that are same, only the slopes differ."

'That's strange!"

"It is Sir, quite unusual," replied Mr. Guest.

"Don't speak about this thing to everyone," Mr. Utterson cautioned.

"I won't Sir, I understand the need for secrecy," the clerk replied.

Soon after Mr. Guest left, the lawyer picked up the two papers and locked them away in his safe. His clerk's observation had only made him more worried.

"This cannot be!" he muttered to himself,

"Why would Henry Jekyll forge a document for a murderer?" A terrible fear rose up in Utterson's heart as he wondered why a man as respectable and good as the doctor would do such a thing.

# Six

# Remarkable Incident Of Dr. Lanyon

The brutal murder of a person as respectable as Sir Danvers caused a lot of public outcry. Thousands of pounds were promised as a reward for anyone who might help in catching the culprit. But time passed away without anybody catching even a distant sight of Mr. Hyde. It was almost as if the person called Edward Hyde had stopped existing. A lot many stories about his evil past crept out however, all proclaiming him a villain and a man of disrepute. People talked about his cruelty, violence, degraded manner of living and all kinds of odd people with which he had associated. But nobody seemed to know anything about his present whereabouts. Hyde seemed to have vanished from the face of the earth.

Hyde's disappearance had relieved Mr. Utterson of his dreadful worries. He hoped that the villain would never return again to haunt his thoughts and his friend's life. The lawyer was glad to notice that Dr. Jekyll was recovering well too and was becoming more like his old jovial self. The doctor was less secretive now and was making efforts to renew his old friendships. He had started entertaining guests and hosting parties like before and even his face looked brighter and more cheerful now.

In fact a merry little party had been held in the doctor's home on the 8th of January. A small group of friends, including Mr. Utterson and Dr. Lanyon as well, had assembled there. They all laughed and chatted just like old times. Mr. Utterson felt much relieved to see Dr. Jekyll so cheerful and merry.

However, all his worries came rushing back to Utterson on twelfth of January when he was denied the entry into Dr. Jekyll's home. The same thing happened on fourteenth and then on fifteenth as well. Each time Poole told the lawyer that the doctor did not wish to see anybody.

All this made the lawyer anxious again, Two days later he went to the home of Dr. Lanyon to discuss the strange matter with him.

At Dr. Lanyon's home he was cordially welcomed. But Mr. Utterson was shocked to see the sudden change which had taken place in the doctor's appearance. He looked like a dying man. He had grown pale, thin and looked balder and older. And yet what arrested the lawyer's attention was a look in the eye of Dr. Lanyon that showed some deep-seated terror of the mind.

Mr. Utterson suspected that his friend had acquired some grave illness and it was the thought of death that had terrified him. "He is a doctor," Mr. Utterson thought to himself, "he must be aware of his condition and know that he will die soon. It must be this knowledge that has made him so scared."

And yet when Utterson enquired about the doctor's health, it was almost as if with a relief that Lanyon declared himself a doomed man.

"I've had a terrible shock that has left me very terrified Utterson," Dr. Lanyon replied. "I fear I would never recover now. Perhaps in just few more weeks you would be mourning my death for I'm sure I won't survive long."

"What is happening Lanyon? Jekyll is sick too and here you too are talking about death! What's wrong?" Mr. Utterson asked.

"Don't talk to me about Jekyll. I neither want to hear anything about him nor to see him ever again. That man is already dead for me and I beg you not to talk to me about him," Dr. Lanyon burst out in loud but trembling voice.

"But Jekyll is our friend Lanyon. Can I do anything? We are three very old friends, Lanyon. We must not quarrel like that," Mr. Utterson asked.

"No, nothing can be done now. You can ask Jekyll himself if you don't believe me!"

"He's not seeing me. I was not even allowed to enter his home," the lawyer replied.

"I'm not surprised to hear that. Well, you'll know about it all one day, perhaps when I'm dead. But I beg you not to talk about this topic any more. If you can talk about nothing else then I request you to leave me alone. I cannot bear to talk about any of this!"

Mr. Utterson went back to his home feeling a lot disturbed now. He had been worrying about Dr. Jekyll but now even Dr. Lanyon had started behaving strangely too. The lawyer wanted to help his friends but how could he when he didn't even know what it was that was ailing them?

Utterson sat down and wrote a letter to Dr. Jekyll to complain of being denied entry to the house and ask about the cause of this unhappy break with Lanyon.

The reply came early next day. The letter that Dr. Jekyll sent him sounded quite grim and mysterious. Dr. Jekyll had declared that there was nothing that could be done to repair the break in his relationship with Dr. Lanyon.

"But I lay no blame on Lanyon," Jekyll had written. "I agree with him that we should never meet again. And I have decided never to meet you as well. But it's not because I've stopped thinking of you two as my most dear friends. I have decided to live a lonely life as punishment for my sins. I've sinned and I have suffered and will suffer. Nobody can do anything about it. All that you can do for me is to respect my silence and my wish of never seeing you again."

Mr. Utterson was shocked and horrified. He could not understand what might have happened to disturb Dr. Jekyll so terribly. Hyde had disappeared long ago. And everything seemed to be going well too. This sudden turn of events baffled the lawyer and he could understand nothing. He might have considered the letter a result of momentary madness or anger. But Dr. Lanyon's condition had convinced the lawyer that something far more dangerous was going on in the life of his two friends.

Dr. Lanyon's condition kept on getting worse. The very next week he became confined to his bed. Fifteen days later, he was dead.

The night after the funeral, Mr. Utterson

took out an envelope from his safe. It was addressed in Dr. Lanyon's handwriting and was sealed with the words "PRIVATE. For the hands of J.G.Utterson alone. To be destroyed in case of his death, UNREAD." The troubled lawyer quickly broke open the seal and took out the contents. It was yet another envelope, sealed and marked with the words, "Not to be opened until the death or disappearance of Dr. Henry Jekyll."

Mr. Utterson did not like it at all. Here again was mentioned the possibility of Dr. Jekyll's death or disappearance, just like in the will. The lawyer had believed that the will had been dictated by Hyde. But here was the dreadful suggestion again, in Dr. Lanyon's handwriting. What could be the meaning of this? Mr. Utterson felt curious and alarmed and wanted to ignore the words on the envelope. He longed to break the seal and see what was inside. But professional honour and his sense of loyalty towards his friends did not permit such a thing. He put the packet back in the safe and walked out of the room.

However, although Utterson had controlled his curiosity, he could not kill it altogether. One of his two best friends was dead, but the other was still alive. The lawyer wanted to talk to this friend and spend time in his company. He went several times to Dr. Jekyll's house. But every time Poole sent him away from the door. The servant told the lawyer that Dr. Jekyll spent all his time in his chamber only. He had stopped going out altogether. Mr. Utterson however kept on visiting the doctor's house, in the hope of being allowed to see his friend again. As time passed on, his hopes died out and his visits became less frequent.

## Seven

# Incident At The Window

M r. Utterson was roaming around with Mr. Enfield on one of their usual Sunday walks. They were just strolling and chatting with each other when they came near the house where Mr. Utterson had once encountered Hyde.

"I'm glad that the story about Hyde is over. I'm glad that he has run away and we shall never see him again," Mr. Enfield said as he looked up at the house.

"I don't want to see him ever again either," Mr. Utterson commented. "Did I tell you how I met Hyde once and felt the same kind of repulsion as you felt? I wonder what it is about that man?"

"Yes, you told me," Enfield replied. "By the way, I just realized that this house is situated just behind the home of Dr. Jekyll.

And in that case, this door must be the back way to the doctor's home!"

"Yes, you are right!" Mr. Utterson exclaimed. "Let us step into the yard. Perhaps we might catch a sight of Dr. Jekyll from the windows. I've not seen Jekyll for so long. I'm worried about him. May be if he sees us, he might relent and invite us inside."

With this thought, the two friends stepped into the cool and damp yard. The sun was about to set but as yet there was light enough. There were no windows on the ground floor. Mr. Utterson looked up at the windows on the upper floor. The middle window was half open and sitting beside it was Dr. Jekyll, looking more sad and sick than the lawyer had ever seen him before.

"Hello Jekyll!" Mr. Utterson called out, "How are you feeling now?"

"Not very well, Utterson," the doctor replied. "I'm feeling terrible. But soon all my suffering will be over," Dr. Jekyll said with an air of extreme sadness.

"Why have you confined yourself like that? You should go out more, I'm sure the fresh air would do you good. This is my cousin Mr. Enfield. We are just enjoying a leisurely walk. Why don't you come out and join us too?"

"That is very kind of you Utterson," Dr. Jekyll replied. "I would like to have a walk with you too. But I can't come out. It's quite impossible. I'm sure glad to you see. But I can't ask you to come in because my home is not fit for you to enter."

"No problem," the lawyer replied. "We can stand down here and talk to you."

"That is a good idea, thanks," Dr. Jekyll said with a smile. But suddenly his smile vanished away and utter terror took its place. The two gentlemen standing below noticed the doctor's sudden fear and became scared themselves. But before they could ask anything, Dr. Jekyll closed the window with quick sudden movements. Utterson and Enfield stared up at its closed shutters for some moments but had no other choice but to step out of the yard and go back on their own way. They walked back in silence, both feeling very worried and scared.

"God forgive us! God forgive us!" Mr. Utterson kept on muttering.

Mr. Enfield only nodded and remained silent.

## Eight

# The Last Night

Mr. Utterson was sitting quietly by his fireside when he was surprised by a visit from Poole.

"What happened Poole? Why have you come here? Is your master very ill?" the lawyer asked immediately.

"I don't know Mr. Utterson," said the man, "but there certainly is something wrong."

"Take a seat," said the lawyer. "Now, calm down and tell me clearly what has happened."

"You know how the doctor has been behaving since last some days, sir," replied Poole, "and how he shuts himself up and refuses to see anyone. Well, he has shut up himself again in his room and I don't like it, Sir. It makes me very scared."

"Now, my good man," said the lawyer,

"tell me clearly. What are you afraid of?"

"I've been scared for about a week," returned Poole. "And I can bear it no more."

The man's appearance clearly showed that he really was terrified. He was behaving strangely and except for the moment when he had first announced his terror, he had not once looked the lawyer in the face. Even now, he sat with his eyes staring at a corner of the floor. "I can't bear it anymore," he repeated.

"Come," said the lawyer, "I'm sure you must have some good reason to be so scared, Poole. I guess there is something seriously wrong. Try to tell me what it is."

"I think there's been foul play," Poole finally declared in a hoarse voice.

"Foul play!" cried the lawyer, feeling a sudden fear rise up in his heart as well. "What foul play? What do you mean?"

"Yes, I think there is some foul play, Sir. I fear somebody is trying to harm the doctor. I don't know much but I would request you to come with me and see for yourself."

Mr. Utterson left his seat immediately and became ready in a minute to go and see his friend. The lawyer and Poole stepped out on the street, Poole looking much relieved. It was a very wild and windy night. The streets were bare and bore a deserted look. The two men soon reached the by-lane. The place was all dusty with the wind blowing about in strong gusts and trees lashing and moaning with the wind.

"Here we are Sir," Poole said taking off his hat and wiping his sweaty brow. "I hope nothing bad has happened already."

"I hope so too, Poole," Mr. Utterson nodded.

Poole knocked and the door was opened immediately by another servant who was looking just as grim and worried as Poole. As the lawyer entered the house, he saw all other servants assembled in the hall like a terrified flock of sheep. A bright fire was blazing warmly in the hall, but none of the servants gathered looked even a little bit comfortable. As soon as they saw Mr. Utterson, they all began to whimper their fears out to him. The cook ran towards him with anguish written clear on his face.

"What's the meaning of all this?" the lawyer asked. "Why are you all gathered here like this? Your master would not like you ignoring your duties."

"They are all just as scared about Dr. Jekyll as I am, Sir," Poole said. A low wail broke out from the maid as he was saying this. "Keep quiet and don't make such noises!" Poole shouted immediately. He ordered one of the servants to bring a candle for Mr. Utterson and then asked the lawyer to follow him through the back garden.

"Please Sir," Poole begged Mr. Utterson as he led the elderly man towards Dr. Jekyll's chambers, "come as softly as you can. I don't want the master to hear you. However, by any chance if he hears you and calls you in, don't go!"

Mr. Utterson trembled a little to hear such fear in the servant's voice. But he did not let that stop him and continued to follow Poole into the laboratory building through the surgery up to the foot of stairs. Poole whispered to the lawyer to wait quietly and listen while he climbed up the stairs and knocked on the door of his master's chamber door.

"Excuse me Sir," Poole said, "Mr. Utterson wants to see you."

"Tell him I don't want to see anyone," a voice answered from behind the closed door.

"Alright Sir, I will let him know," Poole answered and climbed down the stairs. He led the lawyer away back across the yard to the kitchen. "Did you hear that Sir? Did that voice sound like my master's?"

"No! It certainly didn't! It sounded very different," Mr. Utterson replied looking paler than ever.

"Different? Sure it is different!" Poole cried back. "I've served Dr. Jekyll for twenty long years. And yet I don't recognise the voice that sounded from behind that door, Sir!" It cannot be my master's. I fear my master is dead Mr. Utterson! And it's been eight days since he died and somebody else has taken his place since then. I don't know who is in that room or why is he there. But I know that it is not my master!"

"But that cannot be, Poole," said Mr. Utterson. "Even if Dr. Jekyll is dead, which I hope is not the case, why would his murderer linger behind in his room? It makes no sense."

"I don't know if it makes sense or not, what I do know is that *that* voice did not belong to my master. Let me tell you something else too. All last week, whoever is living in that room has been asking for some medicine. He writes his orders for this medicine and throws it down the stairs for us to pick them up. And that's the only communication we've had with whoever is living in that room now. He has not communicated to us except by means of these papers. Even his food is to be left on the top of the stairs which he takes in when no one is there to look at him. That person sends me to some chemist to bring the medicines. But every time I bring that stuff, he throws down another paper saying that the medicine is not pure enough and that I must bring it from some other chemist. I don't know what kind of medicine this is. But whatever it is, the person in that room wants it really badly," Poole said.

"Can you show me any of those papers?" Mr. Utterson asked.

Poole immediately pulled out a paper from his pocket and showed it to the lawyer. The words on the paper read—" Dr. Jekyll presents his compliments to Messrs. Maw & Co. He wants to inform them that the last sample of the drug ordered was impure and is thus useless for the purpose desired. Last year Dr. Jekyll purchased a large quantity from Messrs. Maw & Co. He now requests them to search for the same quality and send it at once. It does not matter how expensive the medicine is. It is of greatest importance that it is pure and of high quality."

"This seems to be Dr. Jekyll's handwriting. It was not written by anyone else," Mr. Utterson said.

"What difference does a handwriting make? I have seen him, the person who lives in that room!" Poole cried out.

"Seen him? What do you mean?"

"Well, it was like this, Sir," Poole began, "I once entered into the surgery from the garden. The person living in that room had slipped out to search for something among the packing cases and crates. His door was open. He looked up at me, gave a sudden cry and ran upstairs into his room and shut the door. I saw him only for a minute but even that was enough to scare me out of my wits. He was wearing a mask, Sir. Why would my master wear a mask? And why would he run away after seeing me? I've been serving Dr, Jekyll loyally for so long!"

"I think I understand the mystery now," Mr. Utterson replied. "I think your master has acquired some serious illness, of the kind that deforms the patient. That might be why Jekyll is avoiding meeting anybody. That can also be the reason behind the change in his voice and the necessity of wearing a mask. Perhaps it is to cure this disease that the doctor is asking for that medicine. I hope he'll get his medicine soon, of the quality that he requires. I hope he'll be able to cure himself soon. That can be the only reason behind his strange behaviour."

"No Sir, the person I saw was not my master. Dr. Jekyll is a tall man, but the person I saw was very short. I cannot be so mistaken Sir! I still believe that Dr. Jekyll has been killed. And I suspect that it was Mr. Hyde who killed him. The person I saw was of the same built as Mr. Hyde and gave me the same creepy feeling that Mr. Hyde evokes," Poole said.

"Well, in that case we'll have to make sure. I know Jekyll does not want to be seen. But I'll break the door if I have to and get to the bottom of all this! Will you help me Poole?"

"Yes, Sir. I'll help you break the door. It might be wrong, but I'll do it," Poole replied.

"Alright, and don't worry. I'll take the entire blame on myself. You won't come to any harm," the lawyer assured. Then he called the footmen and ordered him to guard the backdoor with another of Dr. Jekyll's servant.

In few minutes Mr. Utterson and Poole climbed up the stairs with an axe and a poker.

As they walked up towards the doctor's room, they could hear the sounds of someone pacing restlessly in the room.

"That's just the way he keeps on walking all day, and often all night as well. I guess it's guilty conscience that does not allow him to rest," Poole muttered.

The lawyer listened to the sound of footsteps too. The person seemed to be walking in an uneven and unsteady way. It was very different from doctor Jekyll's firm and steady tread. Poole settled the candle on a nearby table and then approached the door with Mr. Utterson.

"Jekyll, I've come to see you and I won't go back without having a look at you!" Mr. Utterson called out in a loud voice. The person behind the door stopped walking but gave no reply. "I warn you that I suspect something dangerous going on in your life. And I will enter your room, by any way I can."

"Oh, Utterson!" a voice cried out from behind the door, "For God's sake go away! Have mercy on me!"

"That's certainly not Jekyll's voice! It's that horrible Hyde in that room! We must break the door, now!" Mr. Utterson exclaimed.

Poole lifted up the axe over his head and threw a hard blow at the door. A terrified scream rose up from behind the door. Poole kept on striking his axe at the door again and again. Finally, at the fifth blow the lock was broken and the door fell inwards on to the carpet.

Mr. Utterson and Poole looked inside. A fire was blazing in the grate. On the table, several papers were set out neatly. Tea things too were laid out near the fire. Several chemical bottles stood on the stands against a wall. And right in the middle of the room lay the body of a man. Mr. Utterson and Poole tiptoed into the room and turned the body on its back. It was the dead body of Hyde. He was dressed in the clothes that were too large for him, being from the cupboard of Dr. Jekyll. His body was twisted and his face was frozen in an expression of intense pain. His hand still held a crushed capsule. A peculiar smell hung in the heavy air of the room.

"It's too late!" Mr. Utterson muttered. "We can neither save him now, nor punish him. Hyde has killed himself. But where is Jekyll? We must find him, or his body if he is dead too."

Dr. Jekyll's home was a large and spacious building with many rooms, closets and cellars. Major portion of this building was occupied by the surgery and laboratory room. A passage connected the surgery room to the by-lane. All the rooms were thoroughly checked by Poole and Mr. Utterson. However, there was no trace of Dr. Jekyll anywhere. Poole stamped his feet on the paving stones of the passage connecting surgery to the by-lane.

"Can Dr. Jekyll be buried here?" he asked.

"Or perhaps he has simply run away," Mr. Utterson muttered. "Hyde might have terrified the doctor out of his own home!" But an examination of the back door showed that it was shut tight and locked from inside. It looked as if nobody had even touched it for a long time.

"I cannot understand this. There's some very deep mystery here. Let's look once more in the doctor's chambers," the lawyer suggested.

The two men climbed back up to the room where Hyde's body still lay undisturbed. Both Mr. Utterson and Poole started examining the room slowly and carefully. They noticed evidences of some kind of chemical work on one table. They saw several heaps of something like white salt held in glass saucers.

"This is the medicine that the doctor made me bring for him, Sir," Poole said.

Mr. Utterson looked carefully at all the bottles of chemicals and test tubes containing various chemicals and stuff. There was also a burner in the room. "What was Jekyll doing with all these things?" the lawyer wondered to himself.

He soon turned to look at the business table. Several neat bundles of papers lay on it. And among them was a large envelope addressed to Mr. Utterson in Dr. Jekyll's own handwriting. The lawyer lost no time in opening it. As he did so, several documents fell from it. One of these was a will. It was identical to the one that the lawyer already had in his office safe. The only difference was that instead of Edward Hyde, the beneficiary was named as Utterson himself. This meant that in case of death or disappearance of the doctor, all his property was to be handed over to the lawyer. Mr. Utterson stared at the will with utter surprise. Then he turned and looked at the body of Hyde.

"This is getting just too baffling!" Mr. Utterson said. "Hyde had been living here since so many days. He surely had neither any reason to like me nor to consider me as a friend. He must have seen these documents and yet, he had not even tried to destroy them! Why?"

The lawyer soon turned his attention to the other documents that had fallen out from the envelope. He picked up a paper. It was in Dr. Jekyll's handwriting and was dated the same day.

"Oh, Poole!" the lawyer cried out. "Jekyll was alive and here in this very room today!

Hyde cannot have killed and hidden his body in such short time. Jekyll must have run away. But why? And why did Hyde commit suicide? What is the meaning of all this?"

"What has the doctor written Sir?" Poole asked.

Utterson brought the page before his eyes and started reading. It was quite a brief letter that bore these words:

"My dear Utterson,

When this letter falls in your hand, it's most certain that I shall have disappeared. And I have reasons to believe that such a time is not far away. Go and read the narrative that Lanyon has given you. And if you still care to know more, read my confession which is enclosed in this envelope.

Your unhappy friend,

Henry Jekyll."

The lawyer picked up the third enclosure. It was a thick packet of papers, carefully sealed. He put it in his pocket and told Poole not to tell about Hyde's death or Dr. Jekyll's disappearance to anyone.

"I'm going home to study these papers. But I'll return before midnight. Don't do anything till then. We can call the police later," Mr. Utterson said and quickly walked out of the doctor's home.

# Nine

# Dr. Lanyon's Narrative

Mr. Utterson went home and immediately took out the packet that had been sent to him by Dr. Lanyon. He opened it quickly and started reading.

"About four days ago, on the ninth of January, I received an envelope by registered post. It was sent by Henry Jekyll. I was surprised to see it because he had never written a letter to me on any previous occasion. And I had actually dined with him on the previous day. I could not imagine why Jekyll had felt the necessity to send me a letter by registered post. My surprise increased as I read the letter. It ran thus:

'Dear Lanyon,

You are one of my oldest and most dear friends. We have often disagreed with each other regarding our scientific opinions, but

I've always considered you as a friend very close to my heart. I trust you completely. And it is this trust that makes me bold enough to ask a favour of you. Lanyon, my life, my honour and reputation is now at your mercy. If you don't help me, then I'd have no hope left. What I will now ask you to do would appear strange to you. But I hope you'd not fail me.

I want you to take a cab and drive to my home. There, Poole would be waiting for you with a locksmith. I want you to break open the lock of my chamber door and enter into the room alone. In my cabinet, there's a drawer marked 'E'. Pull it out and bring it back to your own home, without disturbing its contents. It contains some powders and capsules and a book.

You should be back to your home by midnight. Please stay in your consulting room at around midnight, alone. A man will come to you in my name. Please admit him personally and give him the drawer that you have brought from my room.

This is very important Lanyon. All this

might sound very baffling to you. But I beg you not to ignore my request. My life, honour and sanity are at stake.

Yours faithfully,

Henry Jekyll.'

'P. S. I had already sealed this up when a sudden fear struck me. It is possible there occurs some accidental delay at the post office and this letter not come into your hands until to-morrow morning. In that case, dear Lanyon, do what I request when it shall be most convenient for you in the course of the day and expect my messenger at midnight. If no messenger comes to you, then you may be sure that it is already too late and that Henry Jekyll is no longer alive.'

As I read the letter I was sure that my friend had already lost his sanity. But I couldn't have ignored his wishes. So I did everything that he had asked me to do. I went to Jekyll's home, broke open the lock of his chamber and brought the drawer marked 'E' to my home.

I examined the contents of the drawer. The powders were measured out into doses.

A wrapped packet contained some salt of white colour. The capsules were half full with a red liquid that had a pungent smell and seemed to contain phosphorous and ether. The book was an ordinary note-book that contained a series of dates covering many years and ending about a year back. Against some dates were written remarks like 'total failure', 'double dose'. I guessed it to be a record of series of experiments. All this seemed very strange and mysterious.

At about midnight I waited alone to receive Jekyll's messenger. At exactly twelve o'clock, there was a gentle knock at my door. I opened it and found a small man leaning against the pillar of the gate.

"Have you been sent by Dr. Jekyll?" I asked him.

The person nodded slightly. I asked him to come inside. He looked around as if fearful of being seen by somebody else. There was a policeman at some distance. Seeing him, my visitor started and rushed inside my home.

I found that quite strange and suspicious and as I followed him into my consulting-room, I kept my hand ready on my gun. In the bright light of the room, at last, I had a chance of seeing him clearly. The first thing that I realized after seeing him was that I had never seen that man before. And the second thing that struck me was the shocking expression of his face.

This person (who had from the first moment of his entrance, struck in me what I can only describe as a disgustful curiosity) was dressed in a way that would have made an ordinary person laughable. His clothes, although they were expensive and good, were too large for him in every measurement. The trousers hung on his legs and were rolled up to keep them from sweeping the ground. The waist of the coat was below his hips, and the collar was sprawling wide upon his shoulders. Strangely however, this ridiculousness of his clothes didn't seem at all amusing on him. Rather, these ill-fitted clothes matched with the person's own abnormality. All this made me very curious to know about my visitor's nature and character, and also about his origin, his life, his fortune and status in the world.

My visitor looked very excited and impatient and asked me immediately if I had brought the drawer.

"Have you got it?" he cried. "Have you got it?" And so great was his impatience that he even laid his hand upon my arm and tried to shake me.

The touch of his hand on my arm sent cold shivers through my body. It was almost as if I had been touched by some vicious spirit. I did not at all like his impatient manners and coolly told him to sit down and introduce himself. The man apologised for his rudeness and sat down. He said that he had been sent by Dr. Jekyll to fetch a drawer. I pointed him towards the drawer. He immediately sprang up on his feet and rushed towards the drawer. His face became flushed, his hand went up to his heart and I heard him gnashing his teeth with feverish excitement. His face became so pale that I felt afraid that he would collapse with too much excitement.

I advised him to calm down. The man

only looked at me and gave me a devilish smile. Then he had a thorough look at the contents of his drawer and gave out a sigh of relief before asking me if I had a measuring glass.

I nodded and brought him a measuring glass. My visitor thanked me and measured out a little red liquid from the capsule and added one of the powders to it. The mixture brightened in colour and started bubbling and giving off fumes and vapours. Soon however the bubbling ceased and the colour of the liquid changed to dark purple and then to watery green. My visitor looked at me with a mysterious smile playing on his face.

"And now Sir, would you let me take this liquid away without asking any further question or are you feeling too curious to let me go away without clearing your doubts? The choice is yours, but think well before asking because the answers may not be necessarily pleasing to you," that wicked looking man said to me.

"All this is nothing less than a strange riddle to me Sir," I answered trying to remain as calm as possible. "I've done all that Dr. Jekyll wanted me to do. I've not come so far to let the mystery remain as it is and not seek the explanations."

"Well then," he replied, "I'll tell you everything but you must promise me that whatever you'll see now will remain a secret with you. You've always bound yourself by narrow and conventional views and you never believed in the existence of supernatural medicine. But now you are about to see something that would make you believe in the existence of Devil himself!"

He lifted up the glass with that strange liquid and emptied it in one gulp. A terrifying cry rose from his throat, he staggered, grabbed at the table, his eyes became bloodshot and he started gasping for breath. And then, right before me the man started changing! He started expanding, his face changed, and his skin turned dark and then light. I sprang up from my chair with shock and ran towards the far wall.

"O God! O God!" I screamed again and again, for there before my eyes — pale and shaken, and half-fainting, and groping before him with his hands like a man restored from death — there stood Henry Jekyll!

I can not tell you the lengthy explanations Jekyll gave me after his transformation was complete. All I can say is that what I saw and heard that night sickened my soul and my body as well. What I saw and heard was too bizarre to be believed and yet, it was all true. It has shocked me too much. I can neither sleep now nor rest peacefully. I'm terrified and feel that this terror would cause the end of me soon. Jekyll narrated to me a tale of moral downfall that is too horrifying to even utter. It has terrified me beyond anything else.

Only one thing more remains to be told, Utterson. The repulsive creature that had stepped into my home that night was, according to Jekyll himself, a person called Edward Hyde. Yes, the very man who killed Sir Danvers Carew!

H. Lanyon."

## Ten

# Henry Jekyll's Full Statement Of The Case

Mr. Utterson could not believe what he read in Dr. Lanyon's narrative. It filled him with amazement as well as shock. He immediately picked up Dr. Jekyll's confession and started reading it. The document made the lawyer even more sad and amazed as he progressed through it. It was the story of Dr. Jekyll's life and the sad misfortune that Jekyll had brought upon himself and read thus:

"I took birth in a family that was rich, prestigious and respectable. God blessed me with good looks, health and intelligence and a will to work hard and attain a life of prestige and honour. I respected and was respected by my fellows who considered me as a man of great future.

At the same time I harboured a secret

fascination for unhesitating gaiety and fun. However, I always felt ashamed of these instincts and tried to repress them as these qualities clashed with my high ideals and higher aspirations. Soon it became a habit for me to conceal and keep secret the things that gave me the real pleasures. I demanded high standards from myself and started feeling shameful about my little faults and pleasures. Before I knew it, I had already started living a double life. I myself became divided into two. One part of me was rigorously good, other unhesitatingly evil. It was not as if I was a bad person trying to pose as a good man. Each side of me was just as genuine as the other. I tried repressing my bad side, but the more I tried hiding my faults, the more eager they became. And this distressed me greatly as I really wanted to be all good and yet could not let go the joys of being bad once in a while.

As my scientific studies were also related to the mystic and supernatural, I soon realized that the man is not made up of a single personality, but is a combination of two. I have understood it now that a person is a combination of good as well as evil. Both these forces exist in a person and it depends upon the individual how to balance them to live a healthy and happy life. Maybe, later studies would reveal it to others too and prove my assertion that man is a complex being of many independent personalities.

I, however, concentrated my research in one direction only. I tried to understand my own duality. The two natures within me struggled to overpower the other and I often wondered how good it would be if I could separate these two parts of me and can be either all good or all bad, as and when I so choose. I felt if I could separate these contradictory personalities in two separate beings, life would become much more simple and bearable. I wanted to separate the good and the bad personalities from each other and set them free to go their own way instead of always struggling to take control of the same person.

As I continued my scientific and mystical studies, I started discovering certain chemical combinations that have the power to remove one nature and give the other total supremacy over the person. I will not give the details of my research. All I can say is that I succeeded in developing a drug preparation that could remove one of my personalities and let the other have total supremacy over me.

I thought long and hard before testing that drug upon myself. I knew it was powerful and if anything went wrong, it could have killed me instantly.

But I knew I had made a great discovery and it was just too tempting not to try it out. Everything was ready. All that was needed was to add to the medicine a certain salt that I had purchased from a chemist. I mixed the salt and watched the mixture bubble and give out fumes. Then, taking hold of my courage, I gulped the medicine down.

A severe pain racked through my shaking body and my soul filled up as if with spiritual horror. But all this agony ended soon and I began to feel a new energy within me, a new vigour and a strange delight. I felt younger, stronger and free from all my responsibilities and moral considerations. It thrilled me to feel wicked and sinful and yet not be ashamed of it. I noticed that I had become shorter in height and lighter in built too.

It was quite late in the night. I slipped out of the room and advanced towards my bedroom, feeling like a stranger in my own home. I quietly entered my bedroom and went straight to the mirror. That was the first time when I saw in the mirror the person you know as Edward Hyde!

Hyde was weaker and shorter than Jekyll because he represented the side of my personality that I had always tried to repress and that, as a result, was less developed, younger and weaker. For most of my life, I had been a good and virtuous person, so naturally the good side of my personality was more advanced than the bad. Goodness shone from the face of Jekyll who represented my good side. Similarly, evil was plainly written on the face of Hyde, the immoral part of my own self.

I know people felt repulsion whenever they

looked at Hyde. But I did not feel any such negative feeling. After all, Hyde was just as much a part of my own personality as Jekyll was. It seemed to me as natural and human and in some ways, more genuine than the face of Henry Jekyll. Perhaps people felt disgusted with Hyde because everybody else is a mixture of good and bad. Hyde, however, was a person who was pure evil.

I had succeeded in separating my bad part from my personality. But I also had to test whether I could revert back to my usual self. I wanted to see if I had lost my original identity for ever. Because in that case, I would have had to run out of the home that belonged to Henry Jekyll and where Edward Hyde could not have been recognised as an owner.

I went back to my study, readied another medicine and drank it up. I went through the same kind of terrible pain again. But within minutes I was once more the old and respectable Dr. Jekyll.

Perhaps I should have tried becoming a person of pure goodness instead of choosing to transform into a person of pure evil. But I never thought about this at that time. I was just too glad to have acquired the power to switch between two identities, one fully wicked – Hyde and the other a normal mixture of good and back as Jekyll.

This power intoxicated me with thrill. I started feeling bored with my life as a normal, respectable old man and hungered again and again to taste the pleasures I could indulge in as Hyde. The things that I could not have dared as Dr. Jekyll for fear of spoiling my reputation, I could do them all as Hyde. Nobody could have imagined that Hyde was nobody else but Henry Jekyll himself, a person everybody considered as an epitome of dignity and morality. Edward Hyde didn't need to fear anybody, because he had no permanent existence. Just one dose of medicine was enough to remove him from the face of the earth and transform him into an aging and respectable doctor whom nobody suspected.

I quickly made thorough arrangements for sustaining this Hyde. I took and furnished a house in Soho and also hired a trustworthy housekeeper. I informed all my servants to consider Hyde (whom I described) as a welcome guest and let him have full freedom of my house in the by-lane. I often visited my own home as Hyde to make myself familiar to them. And then I drew up the will in a way that entitled Hyde to become the owner of everything that Jekyll possessed, in case anything happened to me as Jekyll.

I know Utterson, you considered that will insane. But now you'll realize that *that* was the least part of insanity to which I had surrendered willingly.

I've already told you how I sought rather undignified pleasures as Hyde. But matters soon grew worse. The things Hyde did were not just undignified but monstrous and he did it with not even a tiny sense of remorse. I was often amazed at the level of depravity of a person who was nobody else but a part of my own personality. Hyde was cruel and villainous. He loved to torture innocents and inflict pain and misery on others. I, as Henry Jekyll, often felt shocked and ashamed at the deeds that Hyde did. But it was easy to tell myself that I was not responsible for Hyde's actions. It was easy to believe that Henry Jekyll was still a good person, in no need of feeling ashamed for anything. I soon stopped feeling guilty about things that Hyde did. And if something felt too wrong, I satisfied my guilty conscience by trying to undo the evil deed of Hyde or by compensating in some way.

There were so many cruel and inhuman things that I, as Hyde, committed. I cannot tell you all of them, for there really are too many acts of depravity that Hyde is guilty of. One particular instance I shall tell you Utterson, because it involves your friend Mr. Enfield. It happened one cold night when Hyde collided into a little girl and instead of helping her up, trampled over her and left her crying. Your friend, Enfield, caught me and demanded compensation for the child. I had no other option but to go to the back door that opens up in the by-lane and give them a cheque drawn in the name of Henry Jekyll. That obviously arose some suspicion.

To avoid such instances in future, I deposited a large amount of money in another account opened in the name of Hyde. I also tried to adopt a different handwriting for Hyde by sloping my writing backwards.

I got the first indication of the situation getting out of my control about two months before the murder of Sir Danvers Carew. When I woke up in the morning, I felt odd and had a strange sensation all over me. I looked around, everything was just as usual. But something still felt wrong. A little later I happened to glance at my hand and was shocked to see it turned all dusty, small and hairy. I had gone to bed as Henry Jekyll who had hands that were large, firm and shapely. I immediately jumped out of my bed and ran to the mirror. My blood froze up with terror when I saw Edward Hyde glancing back at me from the mirror. But I had gone to bed as Jekyll! And I had not taken any medicine before sleeping. How could it be then that I had woken up as Hyde? But that was just what had happened.

I was shocked and amazed. But more than

that I was worried that some servant might see me and that might have created problems. But then I remembered that all the servants were already used to seeing Hyde in the house. So I rolled up the clothes I had slept in. They were now too large for me. I hurried to the laboratory, got the drugs I needed and within ten minutes I was once again the normal, respectable Jekyll.

That incident made me think again about what I was doing to myself. I realized that Hyde, the evil part of myself was getting stronger now. I was giving it too much freedom and strengthening the very power that I had kept repressed for so long. I started fearing that I may one day lose the balance between my good and bad parts. Hyde was becoming too strong and I feared that there might come a day when my good self would prove too weak to suppress him. And if that happened, there was a chance that Hyde would become my permanent identity. I had also noticed that the power of the drug that I was using didn't always effect in the same way. Once, there was a total failure and a few times I had to take the double dose too.

It was a terrifying prospect. Once I had battled with the difficulty of freeing my bad self from the good and honest Jekyll. Now it seemed I was losing hold of my original and better self and turning more and more into the vicious person I myself had let out.

The danger was fully apparent to me. I knew that if I kept on entertaining my wicked self, I might one day lose the power and will to turn back to my normal and good self. I had to make a choice. I had to choose between Jekyll and Hyde. These two identities of me had only one thing in common, and that was my memory. But they differed vastly in other faculties. Jekyll, who was a mixture of good and bad, shared and enjoyed the pleasures and adventures of Hyde. Hyde on the other hand did not care about Jekyll. Jekyll was only a body for him to hide in.

Now I had to choose between the two. If I chose to be Jekyll, I knew I would lose the opportunity of indulging in sinful pleasures and adventures which I secretly enjoyed. But on the other hand, deciding in favour of

Hyde would have meant giving up on my career, ambitions and social reputation and becoming a lonely and unsocial wretch instead.

I decided to remain the good Jekyll. I didn't want to risk turning permanently into a person so repulsive that nobody could even stand near him without feeling disgusted and scared. It was much better, I decided, to remain a much honoured elderly doctor who had many friends who loved and respected him. I decided to bid farewell to younger and more daring Hyde and all the activities that I had secretly enjoyed through him. I had made my decision, but evidently I lacked the strength and desire to keep it. Even after deciding to give up Hyde forever, I did not give up the house in Soho. I did not even destroy his clothes.

I managed to keep up my resolution for two months. I remained Henry Jekyll as I had determined. But I missed the freedom and thrill of Hyde. Besides, with the passing of time, my fears of losing my true identity lessened too and temptation increased to try once more the pleasure of being sinful Hyde.

At last, the temptation won. I prepared the mixture again and drank it. Hyde came back, restless and fiery after having being under control for so long. I, as Hyde, was impatient to enjoy the thrill he had been denied for a long time. I walked out of the house, fuming like a caged animal released after long captivity. Wandering around on dark roads, I met an elderly man. The evil in me burst out and I started beating the gentleman for no reason. It thrilled me to see him cry out in pain. It gave me pleasure to see the old man writhe in agony and terror. I enjoyed every blow I gave him. Suddenly the horror of the situation dawned on me and I ran to my house in Soho. I knew I had committed a crime too big to go unnoticed. I destroyed all my papers there and returned to Jekyll's home. I drank the drug and turned back into Henry Jekyll. And this time I knew that whether I liked it or not, Edward Hyde had to go out of existence for ever. The decision was made under the force of the circumstances. Hyde had committed a murder. The only way of his escape and mine as well was to make Hyde vanish forever. There was no other choice left for me. I had to go back to my life as respectable doctor. The very next day it was all over the papers that the man that had been killed was Sir Danvers Carew, a much honoured public figure. Remaining as Henry Jekyll was my only refuge now. Police was looking for Hyde all over the place. There were rewards being offered. There was no doubt in my mind that the moment Hyde came out in public again, he would be caught and punished. I couldn't have risked that.

Once again I decided never again to be Hyde. I decided to remain my normal self for ever and to redeem whatever ills I had already committed. I stopped myself from thinking about the sinful pleasures I could enjoy as Hyde and instead concentrated on seeking pleasure from my friends and my prestigious life.

Unfortunately, it was too late already. I had already given too much freedom to Hyde. He had become too strong. I could feel him getting more and more restless as Jekyll maintained his firm control over him. I, as Henry Jekyll, had no intention of ever even trying to transform into that beast again.

But as I said, things had gone too far already. Hyde had become too strong. He no longer needed the aid of drugs to come out.

It was a very fine day in the month of January. I was sitting in the Regent's park, enjoying the beauty of the weather and feeling thankful for having finally controlled the bad part of me. It was a clear and bright day and birds were singing merrily around. I felt blessed to have escaped the trap of sin and was feeling quite at peace with myself. Suddenly, a shudder ran through my body. An unbearable sense of nausea overtook me. I looked down and noticed my clothes hanging loose around me. My hand became all grimy, dark and hairy. I had once again become Edward Hyde!

I had come to the park as a beloved elderly doctor. But now I had been transformed into an inhuman crook who was being hunted for murder. There was no doubt in my mind that if anyone noticed me, I would be caught and hanged for killing Sir Danvers Carew.

Had I been my good self, I would probably have panicked at the situation. But I was Hyde, and Hyde was cunning and had a sharp and quick mind. Thoughts raced rapidly in my mind and a plan quickly took shape.

The drugs that I needed to turn back into Jekyll were all in my laboratory. I couldn't have gone there as Hyde. My own servants would have caught me and handed me over to the police. I needed someone else to get the drugs for me. The thought of Lanyon came to my mind. I couldn't have just walked upto him as Hyde and asked him to steal a drawer from Jekyll's home. Only Jekyll had the right to ask such a favour. But Jekyll couldn't be back unless he got those medicines.

Then I remembered that even as Hyde, I could still write in Jekyll's handwriting. So I rolled up my clothes, covered my face and got a cab to a Hotel in Portland Street. From there, I sent out two letters by registered post. One requesting Dr. Lanyon to bring that drawer to his home and the other to inform Poole to expect Dr. Lanyon that night and be ready with a locksmith. That's how I arranged to get my medicines from Lanyon's home by visiting him as Jekyll's messenger at midnight.

I drank the medicine in front of Lanyon and turned back into Henry Jekyll right in front of his eyes. I saw the horror on his face. I heard in silence all the condemnation that he showered on me. It affected me deeply and I saw the full horror of what I had gotten myself into.

From that day on, I was no longer afraid of being caught and hanged for the murder I had committed. I was far more scared of turning into Hyde. From Lanyon's home, I had gone straight to my own house. I slept for a long time. That was the last undisturbed sleep that I had. In the morning, I woke up refreshed and felt relieved at the thought of being near my medicine, just in case I needed them again.

After breakfast, I was walking around in my garden when the same pains and shuddering shot through my body. I was Hyde once more. I ran towards my cabinet and had to take a double dose of medicine to become Jekyll again.

From that day, it was only with great effort and regular doses of medicine that I was able to remain the good and honest Jekyll. Again and again, I kept on having those pains as Hyde tried to burst out of me. There was no fixed time. I forever remained in terror of turning into Hyde before the eyes of my own servants. And I couldn't even sleep to relieve my suffering. Because every time I slept or even dozed a little, I always woke up as Hyde. All this was tiring and making Jekyll weaker and weaker. While Hyde kept on gaining strength.

Both Jekyll and Hyde started hating each other. Jekyll had realized the true evil and deformity of Hyde. Hyde was getting more and more restless and hated Jekyll for keeping him a captive. But Hyde knew that if he had to save himself from hanging, he needed the body of Jekyll to hide in. This dependence made Hyde resent Jekyll with even greater intensity. And he also felt afraid of the depression and gloominess that was coming over Jekyll. He feared that Henry Jekyll might commit suicide some day.

Life for Jekyll had become a torture. And the punishment and suffering might have continued for a much longer time perhaps had my stock of salt lasted a little longer. It was the same stock that I had bought at the time of my first experiment. It had lasted me so long but now it was running out. I sent for fresh supplies. But the salt I got this time was not the same one. I mixed it with the medicine, the liquid changed colour once but not the second time. I drank it nevertheless. But it had no effect. I decided that probably the new stock was impure and sent Poole to buy it again from a different chemist. But the result remained the same. In desperation, I sent Poole to almost every chemist in London. But never again could I get the salt of the same quality that I had used in my experiments. Now I believe that perhaps it was the original supply that had some impurity. And it was that impure substance in the salt that had added such magical powers to the mixture.

About a week has passed since I've realized this. I have lost hope of ever getting the same kind of salt that I need. I'm now writing this statement under the effect of the very last dose of my old stock. That means that this is the last time I'm wearing the face of Henry Jekyll. The last time that I'm thinking as Jekyll and doing what he wants to do. This confessional statement and my new will have so far escaped destruction due to care and good luck. I must ensure its safety now. Once I change to Hyde, he will tear away all these pages.

Half and hour from now, I shall forever turn into Edward Hyde. I don't know what will happen then. Perhaps Hyde would be caught and hanged. Perhaps he would kill himself to escape the capture. I don't know. The only thing that is certain is that on this day, half hour later, Henry Jekyll would forever vanish from the face of earth. This is the day of my death. The person who would take over is someone else. And I don't care what will happen to him. Whatever will happen after my death, it will happen to another person not me.

That is all I have to say. I shall now proceed to seal this confession. This is the end, the end of Henry Jekyll's life."